Heart Sticks

Tale of Legend Heart

By Jeff Kraskouskas and Jeffrey Tsui Kraskouskas

Within all of creation, each individual is part of an imperfect whole. Yet within such imperfection, a perfect state exists – one where light illuminates all darkness.

In a remote territory known as the Land of Sticks, deep within subconscious existence, the window of light closed when the androgynous ruler Legend Heart was captured and locked away deep within a mountainous cavern, where the depths of darkness kept all light from the soul. There he was fed a diet of dark matter, a process meant to transform the fabric of the ruler's character until it was unrecognizable.

Black Heart, ruler of Darkness, mused, "The time is now. I shall plunge this land into Darkness, and Legend Heart will be no more, for he will become… Dark Heart." Thus was the devious plan of Black Heart – to transmute Legend Heart into Dark Heart.

Yet a transformation of the soul takes time, and the bricks of darkness must be packed with mortar. For if even a single ray of light can shine in, God's will is possible.

So commenced the era of darkness in the Land of Sticks. Black Heart ruled the populace with anger, greed, and divisive hatred. Before long the hills and valleys of the region grew barren, as light

2

was cornered, confined, and imprisoned by the vibration of darkness. The rivers lost pressure and flow. Lakes dried. Birds fell from the sky. The whole of society became inflicted by a plague of the mind. The majority of the populace, tricked, betrayed, and unable to guard their own hearts, succumbed to darkness and abandoned their dreams.

Life changed. Light found itself banished to a remote region deep within the heart. The bridge to the soul was dismantled, and this deconstruction created a state of opaqueness. The link existing between the heart and soul now teetered on the edge of being snuffed out.

Thanks to the promise of God, some believers yet existed in the darkness. One of these believers was a beautiful girl, the prettiest shade of green you have ever seen. Her smile was vibrant and bright, and it glistened along with her large, illuminated eyes. In darkness, a flicker of light appears bright, much brighter than such a flicker would in a world of light.

There she was in solitude, ever alone, when her flicker of light attracted another. For you see, light attracts light.

A boy approached the flickering light, which now stood almost completely still. It pulled him in closer, until suddenly they were upon one another. Their energies flickered, like flames dancing in the wind. For a moment it appeared the wind picked up, as if Black Heart had turned the fan higher in an attempt to snuff out the flames of light.

The dance of lights continued as the two spirits danced closer and closer. Their eyes met first, attracted to each other's beauty within. The boy reached out his blue toned finger and spoke. "I am Faith Heart."

The girl's eyes glistened with the tears welling up inside them. "I prayed for help with my mission, and you have been sent. This delights me."

As she spoke, Faith became mesmerized. He asked, "What is your name?"

"Hope Heart," she laughed. Her youth was exceeded only by her exuberance.

Within each of them, a link between the heart and soul existed. They were overcome with each other's vibration and fell into a trance-like state, where a dream welled from the seed of nothingness. Such was a godly state, to bring forth a seed from nothingness in a barren land, where the ground is fraught with cracks from drought, where crops were unable to find footing and withered. The populace in the land had turned upon itself, becoming a populace lacking heart, and worse, one on the brink of losing their souls.

It was while they were in this state of mediation that the wind stopped and a subtle voice, as if from the Creator, whispered, "*Hope and Faith...you are chosen...*"

"Did you hear that?" Hope called out.

"Hear what?" Faith asked,

"The message in the wind," Hope said, "Was it just my imagination or did it really exist?"

"It must exist, yes, for we both heard it. We know what we must do." Faith replied.

"We must do it – we must lead the rescue of Legend Heart from Black Heart!" Hope declared.

And in that moment, darkness enveloping them from all sides, the souls and hearts of Hope and Faith combined, creating an illumination.

"We know where he is," Faith said, "We must go."

"Yes," Hope agreed.

They set course for the highest mountain peak in the Land of Sticks. The journey began easily, as their exuberance effortlessly carried them forward. The duo crossed the barren plains and cut around a drying lake bed, a reminder that water quickly becoming a limited resource. They arrived at the steps of the rugged mountain, where only the seeds of God could germinate in crevices and sprout vegetation.

Vegetation was scarce – most could not find footing in the rock mountain. The two travelers looked up, pondering their ascent to the top of the mountain.

"How will we know when we arrive?" Hope wondered.

"We will know," Faith declared, and took a breath. "We will know. The climb is harrowing, yet due to the danger, they rarely have guards positioned along the route. Once we arrive at the stone door, a single robust general stands guard. We will need to trick him, which will be the easy part. The difficult part will be getting the stone door to open. Two ways exist to open the door."

"What are they?" Hope asked excitedly.

"I was in a dream state when a riddle presented itself: *'The way to open the Stone Door is twofold – unlocked from inside, it can be done by one. Outside, by the vibration of thirteen'"* Faith explained, "A strange riddle… what can it mean?"

"The Stone Door can be unlocked two ways: inside by one, outside by the vibration of thirteen. Only two ways to unlock the door…" Hope repeated, "Is that the riddle?"

"Yes… that is how the wind howled in my dream – exactly like that!" Faith mused.

"We have time," Hope suggested, "As we traverse the mountain, we can make sense of it."

Faith agreed, "Yes, we should be able to make sense of it."

Hope and Faith walked step-for-step along the lonely rock path, the only path of its kind, worn down over time. Though the path was born of nature, hundreds of feet had walked upon it since ancient times. Even so, this mountain ahead of them, the fortress of Black Heart, was uncharted due to its ruggedness and venomous vibration.

The wind whispered suddenly, *"Guard your heart."*

"Did you hear that?" Hope asked.

"Guard your heart," Faith and Hope said at the same time.

"Yes," Faith answered, "It means around darkness, you must guard your heart. Do not allow the darkness to penetrate your heart, mind or soul."

The rock path was hidden from view at times, and at others appeared to cut off completely. The duo persevered, fatigued and weary from hiking all day. At last, the trail appeared to end. "This may be the end of the path," Hope announced.

Faith giggled, "How can this be the end of the path? Our journey is an analogy for life. The path ends but always continues. You are Hope Heart – hope for a way! Many times in life or on a journey, you will come to what appears to be the end. For some it will be, yet for others it will be only the beginning."

They stood there, searching for an opportunity. The bare rock was now staring them in the face like adversity itself. Daylight was fading, and Faith warned, "We need to pass this tonight, for if we stay here, we will be exposed to the wind! As day gives way to night, darkness shall surely surround us."

In that moment, Hope made a suggestion, "How about we say a prayer?"

"Prayer?" Faith replied, "Is that mere words, or an action?"

"Prayer is a request to God, made solemnly and sincerely," Hope smiled, "I pray all the time to reveal the unseen."

"An open mind functions best," Faith agreed, and readied to pray.

They stood halfway up a mountain cliff. The howling wind and darkness obscured their view. Hope prayed, "O Lord, O God, bless us in this moment, for in it we surrender to your plan for us. You know what is best. Please send us a sign we are doing your will. Please send a message, or an angel to guide us further along the path. Allow us to understand what we cannot see, and give us blessings and safety in this night. Amen."

Hope's words trailed off, distorted by the howling wind. In the distance, birds flew towards them. Faith counted, astonished, "Thirteen birds now fly to us. The same number of keys to unlock the door. Surely this must be a sign." One of the birds looked different than the others. "One stork and twelve doves," Faith surmised.

Hope and Faith watched the birds slowly approach as they flew against the wind, until the birds finally hovered directly above them. Twelve snowy white doves flew in a v-shaped formation, six to each side, with a stork at the head. The stork spoke to the weary travelers, "The wind whispered help was needed. God creates all things. Nature links the creations. Thus, I am here. How may I help?"

"We need to traverse this rock," Hope exclaimed.

Faith added, "Better yet, we need a lift to the top of the mountain to the spot where a guard defends a stone door."

The stork smiled, "Yes, remember to always be specific in your request. I have seen the guard, and often wonder what he protects. We fly past that direction often enough. I will do my best, yet may not be able to get you to the top, for I lack the strength and endurance to carry you all the way."

Before Hope or Faith could say a word, the stork called to the twelve doves. They circled back as the stork swooped down and lifted the Heart Sticks with his talons. Hope wavered back and forth, and Faith did as well. They were lifted precariously high into the air by the stork. The twelve doves circled beneath them, making a safety net in case they fell.

The wind whistled, but with the guidance of prayer, momentary peace came upon them. They heard a whisper, "*Have peace upon your soul.*"

The stork flew with all his might, passing an adjacent mountain peak and soaring ever higher until exhaustion finally overtook his wings. He spotted a plateau and prepared for a landing in a spot where the Heart Sticks could rest for the night. Darkness enveloped the area, obscuring everything from view. As the stork descended, the twelve doves moved from underneath the Heart Sticks. The sky was now dark, and visibility was poor.

Suddenly, the stork released Hope and Faith into the dark abyss. They opened their mouths to scream, but not a moment had passed before they landed safely on the flat rock only a foot below them. The stork waved wordlessly, and was gone. The stork and the twelve doves disappeared as if they had never been.

"Thank you! Thank you!" Hope and Faith shouted aloud.

Hope thought out loud, "We should rest for the night. In the morning light, we can get our bearings," She paused, puzzling over something. "Did you hear the still voice during the flight?"

In unison, they both stated the same word: "Peace."

Hope described what she had experienced. "During the flight, a vision came to me, that to get the stone door to open, we will need Peace."

Faith concurred, "I felt it too! Weird, it seems as though I felt the message rather than heard it."

They spoke to one another while searching for cover to sleep, eventually finding a rocky corner which offered protection from the wind. Exhausted, they fell fast asleep almost immediately. They slept as if they were ethereal beings, and could not be attacked. As their enemies guarded Legend Heart, God's angels protected them and guided their mission, for their purpose was true and in concert with the Creator's laws.

Cold winds forced Hope and Faith to move closer together. By the time dawn broke, they were nestled as close as can be. They awoke simultaneously and quickly moved away from one another, Faith acting as if he did not know Hope, and Hope acting as she did not know Faith.

Faith spoke, "During the night, something nudged me and kept saying '*Find Peace, find Peace.*' What did they mean? Should I find Peace with you?"

Hope giggled, "You can only find Peace within yourself."

They stopped chitchatting and resumed their mission to the stone door. Hope mused, "At one point, we called it a gate, yet with clarity of sleep we recognize we search for a stone door."

Faith laughed and agreed, "Yes, the gate is a door."

Hope continued, "We search for a stone door and Peace Heart.

Once we find them, the universe will reveal more to us."

"We must keep going," Faith encouraged, "After the initial excitement of a new adventure fades, and weariness looks for a friend in boredom, we must become more obedient and disciplined to reach our goal."

They proceeded around bends in the mountain, traversing a sparse, worn trail until they came upon an outpost. They both knew and simultaneously exclaimed, "This is it!"

They hid from the guard's view behind a rock and paused to catch their breath. From their hiding spot, they looked into the distance, thinking about how they would get to the half-oval shaped door. From a distance, the stone door appeared hermetically sealed, blending together with the mountainside. The door had first been cut, then sealed with fusion, making it impenetrable. For this reason, it was said the door did not need a guard. Even so, at least one guard stood duty most days. Today, a single, large guard sat holding a spear in his left hand. His right hand swatted at the air, crushing an insect.

"How will we distract him?" Hope whispered.

"Let us pray – pray to God now, and in this moment, through the combination of our prayers, the unity of our souls will guide us," Faith reasoned.

The two began to pray together, stumbling over their words. They opened their eyes after a quick, disjointed prayer to notice the guard had fallen into a deep slumber.

"This must be it," Hope suggested.

"Be what?" Faith said.

"Our chance!" Hope replied, and sped without hesitation toward the door, as if not a single fear existed.

Faith hesitated for a moment, but followed expeditiously. "Do we have Divine protection?" he asked nervously.

Hope did not reply, continuing forward as if on a mission, her mind set on the door. She tiptoed past the guard who was now fast asleep, as if a spell had been placed upon him. Faith followed, reaching for Hope's hand and grasping it as they came to the stone door. After a moment's pause, they reached out together to touch the cool stone.

To their surprise, when they touched the door a light blue beam traversed the door alongside a beam of kiwi green. They looked at each other in amazement, wondering what it meant.

Before they could speak, a third color – dark green – raced alongside their lines of kiwi and blue, startling the two Heart Sticks and causing them to look around. Almost immediately, they spotted another Heart Stick kneeling on the ground, touching the door. Hope was lost for a moment as she met the Heart Stick's eyes. Slowly, she moved to speak, but was hushed by their new guest.

In the commotion, the guard stirred, and began to wake from his slumber. The Heart Stick trio scrambled and scattered. They darted in all directions before joining to follow the lead of the new Heart Stick who had touched the door with them. They followed him around the back of the stone mountainous area, away from the door.

The green Heart Stick stopped, knowing they were momentarily safe. Short on breath, he glanced towards his new companions and said, "I am Peace Heart."

Faith and Hope replied simultaneously, "We were looking for you!"

"All say they seek Peace," Peace Heart joked.

"A subtle breeze told us to seek you," Hope explained, "We did not know where to look."

"Allowance," Peace replied, "You accepted it, allowing me to arrive on the scene. Wow, that was exciting!"

"What was?" Faith asked.

"When we all touched the door," Peace replied, "That was amazing, we each unlocked a portion of the door. Wow!"

"What does it mean?" Hope and Faith fumbled over one another.

"It means we can rescue Legend Heart, and save him – save everyone!" Peace beamed.

"You have a beautiful smile," Hope commented.

"Well, when people find Peace in their heart," Peace informed her, "they typically smile, or find it easier to do so, and be content with life. The good news is that with your arrival, we know what we need to do."

"And what is that?" Hope replied.

"We need to find our sister and brother Heart Sticks, or at least certain ones," Peace explained, "Certain ones, who vibrate in our state, and have them touch the door with us. Once we gather all the Heart Sticks, we will all need to contact the door at the same time. If we can manage that, we'll be able to unlock it!"

"Do you really think so?" Faith asked.

"I know so, for I am Peace, and that is why I have waited here, guarding the subconscious of Legend Heart. We cannot allow him to be transformed into Black Heart – we *cannot*." Peace said, a determined look in his eyes.

Faith pondered this new information. "Who else do we need?"

Peace though a moment before speaking, "It looks like we need thirteen, and we have three. For sure I know we need Love Heart and Enthusiasm Heart."

"For sure?" Hope asked for confirmation.

"I am certain," Peace replied, "for without Love Heart, without Love, the door will never open. And without Enthusiasm Heart, Passion will be lost and all the populace will age. For that is truly the definition of old – one who has lost enthusiasm for life."

"We are three, and with those two, we shall be five," Faith summed.

"Yes, oh yes, your math is good!" Peace chuckled.

"Where will we find them?" Hope asked.

"Like you found me, and I found you. We have the power to find all in our dreams, and this is but a dream. We now have Hope, Faith, and Peace. With us three, we can find the remaining ten. We do not know who they all are, but we have faith! Let us have faith that once we find Love, we will find Enthusiasm, and one of them will know who we need to find next," Peace reasoned.

With Peace, Hope, and Love now unified, they descended the mountain in pursuit of Love and Enthusiasm. Initially, they passed the dreary day searching the mountain side left, right, up, down, and everywhere else – to no avail. The mountain was impressive in its sheer size, and had many hiding spots.

They searched for the better part of a day. The slightest movement of a lizard upon a rock had Hope wondering aloud, "Is that Love?"

From a day, the hunt turned into three days, then five. Thirteen days into their search, they were overcome with exhaustion, and doubt began to creep in. The trio sat, resting, wondering whether they had misjudged their efforts to find Love or Enthusiasm. At this point, they would have welcomed finding their half-cousin.

As the search grew more and more futile, Peace sighed, "Perhaps it is not meant to be. Love hides even as we seek."

The trio sat down upon a rock and noticed a dark sky rolling in, as if a storm had a meeting with life. A gentle rain began to fall from the sky, and Hope thought aloud, as if she was full, "We are all full, and it would be a shame, to die full."

"Full, yes, full of our dreams, we must act, and take action in life, for in action we find," Faith erupted. "That is it! We have searched all over this mountainous land, peered in every remote corner we could traverse. We have searched behind rocks, in bushes that moved, near the water, and within the valley. Yet we forgot to search the one place Love is hiding," Faith said, grinning the biggest smile a Heart Stick could grin.

"Where?" Hope asked enthusiastically.

"Inside!" Faith clamored.

Peace chimed in, "Inside the mountain? We cannot get in."

Faith laughed boisterously, "No! Silly Peace. Many have called you silly. You will be the first to die if we do not prevail. Your very life depends on our mission."

The turn in the conversation momentarily sidetracked the main discussion. Peace internalized his thoughts before issuing a reply, "That is not very kind, for you to talk of my death."

"Well, the situation for you is more dire than you know," Faith reasoned, "for if Black Heart succeeds, we will be at war, and peace and war are opposites. You should stay as close to Hope as you can, for she can give you Hope."

"Wow," Hope smiled, "you are very intelligent Faith."

Faith replied, "My intelligence is raw potential. That is to say, my beauty lies in my latent qualities and abilities that vary with each individual."

"Latent?" Peace puzzled over the word.

"Yes, latent," Faith explained, "I am inside of everyone as you are. Though we are powerful, we often times lie dormant, undeveloped. We must develop the qualities we want to become. And *that*," Faith continued, "is the answer to our riddle, to why we have searched for a fortnight without luck." Faith hesitated a moment – freezing as if time had stopped – before blurting out, "Love is inside of us – it has *always* been inside of us!"

Dumbfounded, Hope and Peace looked at Faith Heart, blank expressions across their faces. A silence came over the three as they fell deep in thought, having searched all throughout the mountain and the valley when the answer had lain within themselves the entire time. Though the Heart Sticks knew now what they must do, a new challenge stood before them – they somehow needed to exist in a state of love in order to experience it.

Finally Peace spoke, "We all want love, but that may prove difficult to harness."

"Difficult," Hope agreed, "yet we must try. We must love!" She turned to Faith with his good looks and optimistic personality, his cleverness and his aura of hope.

Peace noticed, and for a second appeared struck with a hint of jealousy, calling out, "Look at me, Hope!"

Full of knowledge, Faith replied, "Hope and I are of the same fabric, like brother and sister, so we have a familial type of love. We all can love in different ways. In fact, the ancients believed there were eight different kinds of love."

Peace's eyes began to well, "What are the eight types of love?"

With a ready answer, Faith replied, "Eros, Philia, Storge, Ludus, Mania, Pragma, Philautia, and Agape."

Hope gasped in surprise, "What do they all mean?"

"Quite simple!" Faith replied, and began going over them one by one. "Eros, or Erotic Love, is where it all starts. Such love is named after Eros, the Greek God of Love and Fertility. Without Eros, society ceases to reproduce and ceases to exist. This love, then, is foundational to the matrix of the universe, and is seen everywhere from animals to insects."

Faith pressed on quickly, "Phillia is affectionate love. Storge is familiar love. Ludus is playful love. Mania is obsessive love. Pragma is enduring love. Philautia is self love, and the final type, Agape, is selfless love."

"Wow…" Hope gasped. She was amazed there were so many types of love. It was as if her eyes and heart had both opened themselves to a new world.

Peace still seemed confused and sat looking at Hope, admiring her beauty. With her smile, vibrant blue eyes, and wavy blonde hair, Hope epitomized the beauty of life.

"Change is a great thing," Faith added, "We must welcome change. Love presents us with a challenge. To find it, we must change ourselves – we must love. Allow us to practice. I have an exercise we can do in a minute that may possibly summon one of the Heart Sticks we seek."

"What is it?" Hope replied, now energized.

"We can summon Enthusiasm within a minute or two by acting enthusiastic," Faith explained, recognizing their own potential lying dormant within. "Here is what we need to do: start acting enthusiastically!"

They began in that moment. Hope started to jump around, and before long Faith and Peace joined in. Once they focused on enthusiasm, it came upon them like rain in a storm. One by one, they began to shout out enthusiastically.

"I'm grateful to be alive!" Faith shouted. He started giggling and laughing, enthusiasm reducing him to a giddy, childlike state.

Peace cried out, "I love life and life loves me! I'm one of the ones who will set Legend Heart free!"

Enthusiasm is contagious, and from the wild scene unfolding, it was more than apparent. The Heart Sticks were dancing next to one another now, interlocking arms and yelling boisterously. Rain began to fall from the sky, as unexpected as the enthusiasm of the trio. Lost in their momentary bliss, rain could not deter their emotions; on the contrary, it only added to them. They each wore broad smiles upon their faces – so broad, in fact, that it was as though a grand, beautiful smile had formed across them, radiating with enthusiasm.

Hope jumped up and down excitedly, "Thank you God for my arms and legs! Thank you for the rain falling from the sky, and thank you for the love in my heart!"

The sun set during this time. The Heart Sticks did not notice, as they were lost in a moment of enthusiasm-inspired pleasure. In moments such as this one, time was meaningless, ceasing to exist. For enthusiasm is a note of music in life that continually seeks to rest. If the musician can hold that note indefinitely, time will stand still.

The excitement and sheer joy of their enthusiasm went on and on, creating a shared connection through their happiness. The trio danced, laughed, and sang aloud; the entire scene was sublime. Then, as innocent as newborn babes, Hope and Peace looked at one another. Their faces, now, were faintly illuminated by a crescent moon, and their eyes danced over each other's soft features. They hugged, then kissed. With the aid of enthusiasm, Hope and Peace fell in love, Faith serving as their witness.

When the two ended their kiss, Hope smiled, repeating what Peace said earlier, "I love life, and life loves me." Then, possibly intoxicated by the sweet nectar of such a wonderful kiss, she continued, "I love Peace, for my heart is full."

Peace was startled yet he, too, fell in love instantaneously, as if he had been touched by something in the midst of his enthusiasm.

Disguised by darkness and the patter of rain, a pair of voices called out from a clandestine source, "You have found us!"

The voices called out again, stronger now. "You have found us!"

It took a minute or so for their exuberance to fade and the noise to subside, and when all was finally quiet a red Heart Stick stood before the group, a brownish Heart Stick standing alongside him. They watched Hope, Peace, and Faith until the three recognized their presence.

Faith noticed them first, and asked, "Who are you noble Heart Sticks?"

Both answered at the same time, though these answers were muffled by the rain. "I am Enthusiasm Heart." Enthusiasm replied.

"I am Love Heart," Love followed.

The voices, together with the distortion of the rain, sounded like, "*LoveEnthusiasm*," or something to that degree.

It took a few seconds for the scene to register before Faith blurted out, "We have found Love, and with a bonus – Enthusiasm!"

Hope and Peace stopped embracing and turned to the other three Heart Sticks. "Where did you come from?" they said in unison.

Innocently, Enthusiasm replied, "From inside of you."

"Why do you jest?" Hope asked.

"Most everyone thinks we exist outside of them – which we do – but to exist out here, we must emanate from a seedling, a form derived from an inner space. We arrived because your inner seedlings of enthusiasm called me out from hiding. And I love companionship, so you will often find me with my friend Love."

And so it came to pass that the rescuers of Legend Heart multiplied, and now five Heart Sticks took up the mission: Faith, Hope, Peace, Love, and Enthusiasm.

They stood in the rain, celebrating their good fortune, realizing they had a real opportunity to rescue Legend Heart. Nevertheless, their task was still daunting. They were now five Heart Sticks, true, yet the Stone Door showed markings for thirteen, with a circle cut in the middle.

Before they could ponder, think, or even analyze their situation, sleep came upon them. They lay in the rain, a warm rain that kept them from being cold. This rain cleansed their collective spirit and renewed their purpose. The five Heart Sticks slept soundly, as if guided by their respective vibrations, the five as one connecting to the source vibration of the Universe.

By the time the sun was peeking its head over the hills the next morning, the rain had subsided. The Heart Sticks awoke, sitting up to watch the rising sun.

Hope was cuddling with Peace as her thoughts left her lips, "We are like the rising sun. We are bearers of light in a world of darkness."

Love Heart came over to them and sat for a moment before speaking. "You two were meant to be together."

"What do you mean?" Hope replied while Peace smiled.

Love answered, "In life, we all hope for peace, so it is fitting that Peace and Hope have fallen in love together."

While the others discussed these topics, and their newfound love, Faith and Enthusiasm stood next to a great Redwood tree, discussing its beauty. They hugged the tree, and tried to touch each other's arms around the trunk, yet they could not. They soon called over the other three in their group, challenging them to see if they could all touch hands while hugging the tree together. The five Heart Sticks stretched as far as they could and were just barely able to touch hands.

They had all begun to pull back from the tree when Faith

suggested, "Let us say a prayer while we hug this great tree."

They all agreed, and hugged the tree again. When they were all touching hands once more, Faith began, "Oh universe, oh great Creator, the odds are four-to-one against us, yet we have your guidance on our side. With your grace and favor, we have everything we need. Thank you for these blessings. Please guide us to the Heart Sticks we need so we might unlock the door and free Legend Heart. His wisdom and virtue are able to transcend time and space. Aligned with nature, we bridge between the portal of this world and that of the Creator. We ask for your help and backing, your favor and grace to successfully complete our mission. Amen."

The group broke hands, and came together a few feet away from the giant Redwood. Enthusiasm spoke up, "We must get ready, for we have more friends to find. Perhaps in friendship, we shall find those we seek…"

"Who do we seek?" Faith asked.

Love answered readily, "While hugging the tree, I had a vision of Grace, Joy, and Happiness. Perhaps it is one of those three we should seek?"

"Yes," Faith agreed, "that sounds right! Let us go forth and seek this trio, for in seeking we shall find them, or at least one of them."

They were at the base of the mountain, and decided to walk the valley for answers, knowing the valley path was safer and less arduous. After a group discussion, they all decided that this path felt right, reasoning Joy and Happiness would be hiding somewhere in this land. But Grace…where could she be?

Hope spoke, "I heard Grace is beautiful. I always wanted to meet her."

"Who told you that?" Peace asked her.

"Every women has heard this," Hope replied. "Grace has always been described as simple elegance and refinement. Her every move appears simple and deliberate. It is who she is."

"Grace will be pleasant to find," Enthusiasm chimed in, "but I question why we walk the lowlands for Joy and Happiness when they exist everywhere – not just in the lowlands."

The words Enthusiasm spoke were not heeded or even heard, but were instead swept up in a breeze, and carried off through the valley, transcending space and time.

The group walked in silence, past sycamores and great oaks, beyond abandoned shelters and desolated areas. They saw birds fly high and low while a flurry of animals scurried to and fro, yet they could not find the Heart Sticks they searched for. Eventually, they came upon a village with shanty abodes and poor living conditions.

As they walked into the village, they found sticks wearing sadness upon their countenance, and others out in the streets making haste of waste. The village sticks looked at Hope, Peace, Faith, Love, and Enthusiasm as if they were from another planet, another world, another universe. One of the village sticks approached and asked, "You are similar to us, yet so different. How can this be?"

The question came abruptly, and without so much as a greeting. No "hello", "how are you", or "my name is...", just a simple observation of the difference between them. A spokesman for the group said, "Here we are, ninety-seven percent of us sticks. You lot must be the other three. We are the village sticks."

The five Heart Sticks had not chosen a leader, or even a formal speaker for their group. Each looked at the others, trying to decide who would answer when Love spoke, "In our hearts, we are all the same."

"I see difference," the village stick said in disagreement. "We do look similar, but we feel different."

"We feel like one of you," Hope said, attempting to soften the village stick's demeanor. As she spoke, however, a group of other village sticks began to form, encircling the Heart Sticks.

"Have we done something wrong?" Enthusiasm questioned, feeling uneasy.

The village stick gave his answer, "We want what you have."

"What do we have that you want?" Faith asked nervously.

"What do you have?" the village leader retorted.

"We have no material possessions," Faith answered, "Do you seek our internal gifts or external?"

"Your external possessions," the stick leader demanded. "Who needs your internal ones, besides your organs?" he added with a crass laugh.

"We do not have any possessions for you," Faith replied for a second time.

"You better find some," the stick leader warned, "or you will be our prisoners."

By this point, the village sticks had surrounded the Heart Sticks on all sides, inching closer in a show of force. "What should we do?" Hope whispered.

Faith, Hope, Peace, Love, and Enthusiasm stood there for what seemed like ages, pondering their predicament. The village stick leader remained firm, motioning for the circle to close tighter around the Heart Sticks.

"What should we do?" Hope whispered a second time.

This question prompted Peace to step forward and ask, "What can we give you that will make you happy?"

The village stick leader dismissed the question. "We do not wish for happiness. We wish for your possessions."

"Most of our possessions are internal." Peace replied, gesturing to demonstrate their lack of worldly possessions. "If it is riches you desire, we can show you the way to riches."

"Yes, it is riches I desire," the village stick leader confirmed.

"The way to be rich is through right living, obedience, discipline, and self-control. Once you receive these gifts, the world shall be yours," Peace preached.

"Hogwash!" the village leader spat, "One of you has a material possession, and to leave you must exchange it for your freedom."

"It is not that simple," Peace pleaded.

The village stick snarled, "To me, it is that simple."

They stood at a silent stand off for minutes, without a word. Each Heart Stick glanced at the others, knowing full well that if any of them had a personal object to trade for their safety, it would be an easy swap to make. The village sticks closed the circle another step, forcing the Heart Sticks to crowd in until they all were within an arm's length of one another. They crowded closer still until they could smell each other's breath. "Well, what is it going to be?" the leader of the village sticks asked, adding a final warning: "This will be the last time I ask. After that, the lady will be first."

Peace Heart spoke quickly with Love Heart right behind him, as if their words were in unison, "Take me first, for she is a lady!"

A village stick laughed, "Ladies before gentle-sticks."

"I see your weakness," the leader proclaimed, "you love!" He directed the mob to step closer. By now they were several rows deep, and the closest ones could nearly reach out and touch the Heart Sticks. One more step and they would surely be able to reach out their arms and grab any of the five they wished.

Cornered and without a good plan, Love directed the others to turn and make four corners facing outward. To protect Hope, they moved her into the middle of their tiny square. Peace looked north,

Faith peered south, Love looked to the west, and Enthusiasm to the east. In this ordeal, Love showed leadership, speaking calmly and confidently for the group. At first, it looked like what Love was saying could be mistaken for gibberish, but soon became clear to the others that she was praying. "Oh God, please protect us in this hour of tribulation. If you have a messenger for us, please send them now, for we are open to your will. Amen." Then Love instructed the Heart Sticks, "Close your eyes, and ask for God's favor."

All five Heart Sticks closed their eyes, preparing for the unknown. Hope stood in the middle, occasionally opening her eyes nervously. Love implored the Creator, "God, please grant us favor even if we have sinned, for in our time of need we now ask for your mercy and grace."

Faith prayed aloud, "We trust in you God, and in our greatest challenge, we see your greatest good." Then he closed his eyes. "May the Holy Spirit be with us and in us."

"Capture and kill!" the village stick leader commanded, angered by the utterance of God. He ordered his army to take their final step to touch the Heart Sticks, who remained praying with eyes closed, fully knowing no possession existed and that they could not give what was asked. A village stick reached out and grabbed the arm of Peace Heart.

At this first touch of Peace Heart, a voice, soft and yet somehow powerful, spoke, "Cain!" The voice echoed as it spoke, as though it emanated from more than one source.

The two voices called out firmly this time, "Cain!" The word could not be ignored; it was crisp and clear as the voices spoke again, "Cain!"

The leader of the village sticks, furious at this interruption, finally replied, "What? What do you want with me now?"

"Stop it now, Cain," the voices said as they moved closer. The Heart Sticks were still praying, and kept their eyes closed.

"Not now!" the voice of the village stick leader called out, "I am busy, and you have been away so long. What gives you the right to barge in on me now?"

"There is no right in your wrongs," the voices answered. "Stop this – immediately!"

"Oh, if you were not my ill twin sisters, life would be different… yet somehow, someway, you have great power…" With that, Cain told his army to step back. The village sticks released their grip on

Peace and took a few steps back.

The voices rang out again, "Allow us access, and free our friends."

Cain screamed, exasperated, "Mercy and Grace! It figures these are your friends. Oh, why do you have friendships with the most pious? Sometimes I wonder how you two could possibly be related to me. I only spare you because you are my sisters. After all, you know what I did to my only brother…"

"The world knows Cain. Your jealousy is second to none," the two voices said in unison. "And we are sure you would try the same with us, but for your knowledge that we are protected on this occasion by a Higher Power."

"Oh Mercy and Grace, why?" Cain shouted aloud. "And who is that with you, that mute who does not speak a word?"

"That is our friend, and what is it to you? You care not for any of our friends," Mercy and Grace replied together. "Allow us to see our friends. They came to this village to see us."

And with those words, Mercy and Grace parted the village sticks. They did not walk toward the five Heart Sticks who were still praying, but instead spoke firmly. "Faith, Love, Hope, Peace, and

Enthusiasm, walk to us."

Faith opened his eyes first, and the others soon followed. They were surprised to see a path parted for them by Mercy and Grace, who none of them knew. The Heart Sticks had only learned the names of the sisters from Cain's banter with them.

"Yes," Faith answered.

The five cornered Heart Sticks walked past the army toward two of the most beautiful Heart Sticks any of them had ever laid eyes on. The third Heart Stick stood in the middle of Mercy and Grace and said nothing. United at last, the eight Heart Sticks now stood together.

Mercy and Grace called out, " Thank you, Cain. We love you."

Cain shouted angrily, "One day, I may summon the courage to kill you, my twin sisters, and lie about it! For you have wasted my time today." He ordered his gang to retreat, lamenting, "Militia, go. Set fires and drink. That will cure our hunger for blood." And so they departed.

The eight Heart Sticks stood together. The twin sisters introduced themselves. The first twin began, "I am Mercy. Your prayers sent me." The other twin continued, "I am Grace. Your prayers sent me as well."

Together, Mercy and Grace explained, "And this is Silence Heart – most call him Silent. You summoned him because he is the definition of strength. It was your silent prayer that defeated the army of Cain. It was Silent Heart who came and awoke us from our beauty sleep."

Hope spoke, "You are as beautiful as they say, and as it is written."

"Who are you?" Mercy and Grace spoke in unison.

"I am Hope Heart," Hope replied.

The other Heart Sticks followed with their own formal introductions. Peace, Love, Enthusiasm, Faith introduced themselves to Mercy, Grace, and Silence.

"Will you join us to free Legend Heart and help restore light to dark souls?" Faith asked the three newcomers.

"Yes," Mercy and Grace said together. Silence concurred by nodding his head up and down.

Under the setting sun, fires burned off in the distance. The Heart Sticks numbered eight now: Faith, Hope, Love, Peace, Enthusiasm, Mercy, Grace, and Silence.

"What is next?" Faith asked.

Mercy and Grace had a habit of speaking together, their words in harmony, and they were always with Silence, or as some called him, Silent. Throughout the land, in tales and stories passed on from generation to generation, it was always said that Silence was the luckiest man in the entire region. Heart Sticks would question how an average Heart Stick like Silence would always be by the side of the two most beautiful twins in the land, Mercy and Grace.

Mercy and Grace had the softest smiles, and beautiful translucent eyes that morphed between the colors of blue, green, brown, yellow, red, purple and orange. Sticks would often not recognize Mercy or Grace when in their presence because rumors held they had blue eyes, and blonde hair, which was not always accurate. Their hair often changed colors, from red to blonde, pink to green, purple, brown and black, and became straight or curvy, curled, or even teased depending upon the seasons and vibrations of the moment.

For all their beauty, Mercy and Grace lived mostly in solitude with Silence. They were not lonely. The populace thought they were too beautiful to associate with, too delicate, already taken, and had so many other misconceptions of them. The twins lived a quiet life, and typically waited for God's call to go where they were needed.

"Next?" Peace pondered out loud, "What is next?"

Hope answered, "The stone door showed thirteen key markings, with a circle in the middle. We still require five more Heart Sticks to open it."

"Who are these five?" Peace asked, "What is the purpose of the circle?"

Enthusiasm chimed in, "Joy and Happiness? It would be great to see them, and they could certainly help!"

A discussion started, the Heart Sticks contemplating who would be needed to help them unlock the sealed stone door. They discussed the possibility and probability of a variety of scenarios and outcomes. They spoke of the twin brothers Desire and Ambition, the cousins Resolution and Industry, the best friends Order and Cleanliness, the twins Temperance and Moderation, and even debated if sages like Humility and Tranquility were needed.

After much discussion, Faith had an idea, "How about we ask and act?"

"What do you mean?" Love replied.

Faith continued, "We can ask the Universe, and wait to hear the answer."

"What if a Stick does not believe in God?" Enthusiasm asked.

"Many do not believe in God," Love replied. "Whether one believes in God or not does not lend clarity to existence, nor does it confirm the powers and laws of the universe."

"In a book they had us read when we were younger," Faith said, "it said ask, so let us ask?"

The eight Heart Sticks agreed, and asked at the same time with the same intentions, "Who are we looking for?" then asked, "What should we do now?"

Just then an elderly Heart Stick passed by the group, a leaf upon his head for hair and a worn out body showing his best days were long past. He came up to the group and spoke, "Why are you paralyzed with fear?" He paused a moment, then answered the question himself. "In life we must act."

"What if we are unsure of our plan?" Hope replied to the elder Stick.

"If you wait for the plan to be perfect, you will grow old like me," the elder Stick began before being interrupted.

"What is your name?" Love asked.

"If you must know," the elder Stick replied, "my name is Broken. So, as I was saying, if you wait for the perfect time, perfect moment, perfect day, or even just the perfect scenario, it may never come, and you will end up like me. My best years have passed me, and I look back wondering, if only I had acted, if only fear had not paralyzed me, if only I would have known I did not need the perfect plan. That if I acted, the plan may have worked out perfectly. Let me call a friend over," Broken said, and he whistled with his fingers in his mouth, a shrill whistle, loud and clear.

A few moments later, another elder Stick showed up and saluted, "Hi Broken."

Broken saluted back, "Hi Regret, you have been a great friend of mine all these years. If it was not for your friendship, I do not know how I would have made it through, or made it this far."

"Yes, we have experienced good times, commiserating by fires, and losing our way at the slightest challenge. We were perfect mates, and we are still best friends." Regret confirmed, "Why do you whistle for me this day?"

"You know the promises I have made, for one more chance, one more dream, so I was summoned by the wind to this place, for these weary travelers do not know what to do next." Broken explained.

"Oh, yes. And what is my role in this? What do you ask of me?" Regret questioned.

Broken smiled, tears in his eyes as he recalled some past pain. He thought a moment before he spoke. "What could have been but never was. You comforted me all these years," Broken explained, "and sometimes my message is lost as I am unable to articulate. Will you help to answer the question these Heart Sticks asked of God? I mean, the Universe." He quickly corrected himself, but it was too late.

"You know I do not believe in God," Regret said.

"Yes, I know. We know. Everybody knows your disdain for God, the word God, and anything godly. You will ignore evidence of God as if you will live forever," Broken explained.

Regret laughed, "But that is my curse – I *will* live forever, or at least until one expresses self-forgiveness. Yes, in most instances, I live forever. But I need company... why should I help these Heart Sticks?" Looking around, he counted, "One, two,...eight! Why should I help these eight?"

"No need to help," Broken prodded, "just be yourself."

"That I can do," Regret clamored. "I would stay right here, and live with you. That will make us all happy, or at least me," he said to the eight, not caring to be introduced or know their names. These ones may have looked different, or perhaps acted differently from others, but it mattered not. For Regret, it was all the same.

Regret continued, "I have more friends than anyone I know, and by no small number. What do you want me to tell this group?"

Broken interrupted Regret's ramblings. "Heart Sticks, go and prosper. Complete your mission. You do not want to end up like me, living life with only Regret to comfort you. Here is my message: ask, which you did, and go on as if it were your last day. Do not concern yourself with what you cannot see. As long as you believe and feel the spirit rest within you, you can go forth without hesitation."

The advice felt right to the Heart Sticks. In unison, they half-bowed, thanking Regret and Broken for sharing promises unfulfilled. They started on their journey. Mercy, Grace, and Silence kept to themselves, not speaking much or often. Hope, Peace, Love, Enthusiasm, and Faith conversed, casting glances at the birds, trees, leaves, stones, and other objects that came into their view.

They walked away from the village sticks. When they were far enough away that their conversation could not be heard, Faith spoke,

"Our plan is to return to the door, knowing we need thirteen Heart Sticks to unlock it."

"How do we know?" Love asked, giggling. "It seems everyone always asks me that question: '*How do we know Love?*'"

"And how do you answer? What do you tell them when they ask?" Peace asked curiously, fresh with a strange feeling upon every fiber of his being about Hope.

Love smiled, "I am one with nature, a force of nature. Therein lies my beauty, my alignment with nature. For you see, I am free. You cannot buy, sell, or trade me. I have no territory or borders, and cannot be contained, only allowed. I am no substance or commodity. You cannot trade me. You cannot imprison me, legislate me, or force someone to feel me. Yet once I strike, it is like lightning – unpredictable and irrefutable. You can choose to surrender to me or not, but when struck, one will undoubtedly feel me even if they do not understand what they feel."

"Wow," Peace commented, having listened intently to Love's speech. "Like my feelings for Hope... why did you strike me?"

Love only giggled in reply, and did not answer.

They walked past a brier patch, whereupon hearing the chirp of a bird within, they glanced deeper and saw reproduction in process. The mother bird sat upon her eggs.

"Now that is me," Love said. "Universal, everywhere, or at least potentially everywhere. The mother expresses me to a child so, in every action she takes to care for her young – feeding them, keeping them warm, helping them develop until they become independent. Then, even when they are beyond her reach, she still hopes for them every day of their existence, thinking of those children as an extension of herself. Truly, I am universal."

Hope smiled, "Yes, like lightning. Natural and unpredictable."

They continued on until they arrived at the base of the stone mountain. "What do they call this mountain?" Enthusiasm asked.

"It is often referred to as Black Stone Mountain," Mercy and Grace replied succinctly.

As they trekked along the base of Black Stone Mountain, Peace offered up a question, "Here we are. Should we make the climb to the Stone Door, or continue to look for the remaining Heart Sticks?" Peace looked deep in thought for a moment before he continued. "We know we are five short. What is our most prudent course of action?"

Faith assumed a position of leadership and spoke to the group, "Prudence is my friend. We have been colleagues in past endeavors. We heard the omen of Broken and Regret, and we need to believe that if we arrive, the rest will. Allow us to call them to where they need to be. Together, with our combined power, we will direct them."

At the base of Black Stone Mountain, Faith directed the eight Heart Sticks to make a circle and hold hands, putting their right hand in the left of the Heart Stick next to them. They closed the circle as directed, Faith holding the left hand of Enthusiasm, who held the hand of Love, who held the hand of Hope, who held the hand of Peace, who held the hand of Mercy, who held the hand of Grace, who held the hand of Silence, who completed the circle by holding the left hand of Faith.

"Allow us to close our eyes momentarily. To prepare, clear all thoughts from your mind," Faith instructed. They stood quietly, doing their best to cleanse their collective minds.

A minute passed, then two, then three, before Faith said, "Allow us to pray for ourselves and one another." This prayer became known as the prayer of Faith:

"Oh Universe, hear our voice, feel our hearts and souls. Our thoughts will define us and your creation through us. We have joined forces and vibrations for your good, and as we look up at the mountain, we recognize this is a parable for life. Though we are short the resources we need to unlock the stone door, we remain faithful and fruitful. Now, in this moment, if we are lost please find us, and bring our Guardian Angels together in council to aide our path and protect us. Thank you God. Thank you, Universe, for our good fortune. Thank you for our safety. Thank you divine intelligence for guiding us. Amen."

"Thank you," Love said to Faith, in response to his prayer, and the Heart Sticks took the first step up the mountain.

Enthusiasm inquired, "You mentioned God in our prayer. What if I do not believe in God?"

Peace laughed, "What do you believe in? He mentioned our Guardian Angels. Do you believe in them?"

Enthusiasm was quick to answer, "Well I came for success, and that is independent of Gods and Angels."

"Do you believe in Joy?" Faith asked.

"Yes." Enthusiasm uttered.

"Do you believe in discipline?" Faith pressed.

"Many times I am unbridled." Enthusiasm said in reply. "Discipline is not my core."

"Is it not your core?" Faith answered, "Or have you deviated so much from your core, that all you know is not as it is and that is why you cannot feel your Guardian Angel or hear the whisper of God? I myself am a fraternal twin. Do you know what that means?"

"You are a fraternal twin, Faith?" Hope asked.

"Yes, we were dizygotic in creation, meaning we came from two eggs and one sperm. Since we have spoken of God, my fraternal status must be mentioned. For one does not need to believe in God to believe in me."

"What do you mean by that?" Enthusiasm peppered Faith with questions, intrigued but confused.

"Many people only see one of me – Faith. They always associate me with religion or God," Faith answered. "Yet in the womb of the Universe, our eggs were dizygotic. The sperm of the Father, and the eggs of Mother Nature."

The lively banter made the early stages of the hike pass by quickly, and the Heart Sticks remained engrossed in the discussion as they pressed on. As they exited the lowlands and began climbing the stone path to the sealed stone door, the vegetation grew less and less. No one noticed a snake slither past, all intent on learning the history of Faith.

Faith continued, "That is why some people say I am a she, and others a he, for in fact I am both. This is also why I have the softness and delicateness of a female, yet retain the strength of a male. For I always travel with my twin, though some choose to neglect one of us or the other."

A warm breeze began to swirl this way and that, directionless, every now and then bringing a drop or two of mist their way. There was just enough mist in the air to make it seems like it might rain, yet the precipitation never came.

"If we are to find the last Heart Sticks to unlock the sealed stoned door, we may need both myself and my twin. Let me explain. Most people associate me with God, for I am godly. Yet my twin was given as a gift from the Creator, who made us two faces to the same body – the body of Faith. The first of us, as I mentioned, is Faith in God, which some believe in, and some do not." Faith explained, "The second and lesser-known of us is Faith in Self."

50

"Both Faiths are you. Of course!" Mercy and Grace said. "Many of us Heart Sticks are twins."

"Yes, that is my lot in this dimension, for that is all that we are: vibrations that come to existence. He is Faith in God, and she is Faith in Self – or was it she is Faith in God, and he is Faith in Self?" Faith meandered, "You see, it can get pretty convoluted. Me and my twin have over time seemingly become one, but as Enthusiasm says, he only sees one of us – Faith in Self."

"Wow!" Love exclaimed, "I never knew any of this about you, Faith."

"Many do not know much about any of us. They call upon us, summon us, talk about us as if we are a novelty, yet they never truly want to know you, Love, or you Hope, and definitely not you Peace!" Faith explained. "That is but one beauty of life, to exist and be unknown, waiting for the world to know you."

"Fascinating!" laughed Peace. "You articulate my struggles. Yes, many neglect me as if I was a novelty act at a carnival, or had two heads. They feel they can do more with a weapon than with me. Such is my lot, yet I endure."

"Yes, to unlock the door, we will need more friends. Will

51

Endurance be one of them?" Faith asked.

They were all deep in thought, pondering who would be needed to help them, yet they remained short on resources. It was noted that Faith traveled with them, so they focused on him for guidance. After learning about Faith, the group became preoccupied with learning about one another. As they progressed, the path turned left. They did not notice until it was almost too late, but the hiss of the snake blocking the path caught their attention as it coiled and lunged at Faith, just missing the Heart Stick.

"The path is blocked by the snake!" Enthusiasm shouted.

"This is an omen," Hope said. "We should use the other path."

"But the other path is more treacherous!" Love replied.

"So it is written!" Peace exclaimed. "So it is said! It is the story of my life. War always says my path is more treacherous. The important thing is we agree the snake is an omen, and we must recognize it. The other path will add a day or two on our trip, for the righteous path always seems longer, and more arduous. In contrast, one can find evil easily, and in quantity."

Heeding the omen, the group changed directions. They knew where they needed to go, but were unsure of the exact path that would take them there. At a loss, the Heart Sticks backtracked, seemingly moving backwards for a short time before heading to the northwest. They soon came upon a plateau with beautiful flowers of pink, yellow, and light blue seeded in rock crevices, with a spring of water in the middle of a meadow. Thirsty, each Heart Stick drank from the spring and, finding the water refreshing, drank some more to revitalize their spirits.

"What a pleasant surprise," Hope cried out, "to find this spring!"

They knew water would be scarce as they ascended the Black Stone Mountain, so they drank to contentment and laid down to rest. When sleep came upon then, it was as if they all were one body falling asleep. All fell asleep at once, and soon a shared dream transpired between them. In the dream, each Heart Stick's respective Guardian Angels stood before them.

It was as if there was only one angel, yet to each Heart Stick, the guardian appeared unique. The figure was dressed differently for each, and upon closer examination, smiled differently for each of them as well. The Guardians were eight strong, yet they all moved as one. Slowly, the Guardians began to speak in unison. "Along the way, you will confront fear, anger, jealousy, hate, greed, and many more ill-suited obstacles. These are the monsters that will attempt to keep you from your dreams. You must not give in. No matter what, hold fast to your dreams."

The Guardians continued. "This is the story of the Dreamer who died with the dream still inside. We Guardians can only help you align, nudge and push. Yes, we will lead you in the direction of the dream. As we are Guardians, we shall protect you, pushing you in the direction the light has placed inside your souls from birth."

"Many will call you fools, and say the soul cannot be quantified. This is great fortune for you all, for science will soon duplicate your brain, and robots will be able to exist without a heart. We will then be able to truly understand how quantifiable the soul is," the Guardian Angels preached, "but we digress. We were discussing our dear friend Dream Stick. Everyone knew of him or her, for each was of a different appearance and a different dream. Yet at the same time, they were all dreams."

"Dream Stick came to a time and to a point," the Guardians continued, "where the dream was built in his heart, imagination and mind – even inside his very soul. We watched and waited, but the Dreamer never acted upon the dream. We saw this happen again and again. Many of the dreamers became distracted or got lost in their responsibilities. Most succumbed to confrontations. When fear confronted them, they became fearful, often because their mind was not right."

"When monsters come, you must be ready to kill them," the Guardians boomed. "We nudged the dreamer, and left tools within his reach."

"Yet the dreamer never picked up the tool," the Guardians intoned. "The dreamer visualized, witnessed, and knew what was possible. They had only to pick up the pen and write, or put hammer to the chisel in his hand and sculpt. They could not. So it was that life moved on and Dream Stick died, unfulfilled and left with nothing but regret. If only the dream had been acted upon! We see this every day, sticks dying with the dreams still inside them. This is a tragic death most do not see. Those looking on see these stick and say '*What a full life they lived!*', yet without action the dreamers' lives are left unfulfilled."

"This is the story of the dreamer who thought through their dream. Though their dream emanated from their soul, they were unable to act with the chisel and the hammer, so their dream died with them." the Guardians concluded, "Go, and unlock the black stone door – circumstance does not matter. The important thing is to know you must go. And once you lay hammer to the chisel, you will sculpt the life of your dreams."

The Guardian Angels disappeared as quickly as they came, blowing trumpets on their way out, celebrating the dreamer who acts, and mourning the dreamer who dreamt without action.

It was morning, and the sky was dark. The moon was full, illuminating the early morning hours. All eight Heart Sticks awoke simultaneously. They each began to speak (with the exception of Silence) – one as seven, and seven as one, similar in fashion to the Guardians they had just seen. Each of the Heart Sticks had witnessed a different Angel, for they were each different spirits assigned as their own Guardian.

"We must act on our dreams," they spoke together. Then they rose, and started hiking up the mountain.

Hope spoke, "We need four or five more friends to unlock the door. At first, I thought Dream Stick would have been one of them, but after last night it seems it will certainly not be my purple friend. A dream without action is just a dream."

They all concurred, shaking heads in agreement. The Heart Sticks were much quieter than usual this morning, in part due to the arduous journey ahead, but more due to the fact they all were now internalizing their own dreams. Would their dreams die inside them, never able to arrive upon the slate of the universe?

Prior to leaving the meadow, they had filled their canteens with water. After three hours of climbing straight up, the group looked tired. They had hit the proverbial first wall. The Heart Sticks rested, drinking from their canteens as they looked for signs and omens.

In a far-off tree a bird crowed, welcoming the new day.

"How long do you think it will take us?" Enthusiasm asked.

Faith replied, "Do not allow such thoughts, Enthusiasm! Be who you are at the core of your being, for Enthusiasm cannot be a slug – it can only be Enthusiasm."

"Time is eternal for me," Love lamented.

Faith continued to step up as the leader of the group, possible due to his zygotic abilities, drawing from the dual faiths of God and Self. Now he encouraged the others, saying "Time is but an illusion that will prevent dreams from happening. For one person will be too old, or the other too young."

"That reminds me," Peace spoke up, "they have told me my whole life that the time is not right. That the time will never be right. We must seize the moment. The time seemed right, but one side was wronged by the other's words, or some other transgression, real or fabricated, would put two forces at odds with one another. Now, the time is right."

Faith commended these words. "Well said, my brother Peace. The time may never be perfect, but it will always be right. We must seize this opportunity."

They continued to hike upward, noticing a large eagle which they took for an omen. The eagle flew near them, making the call of an eagle, faint, weak and choppy. For such a large bird, the faint call was surprising. The eagle's call caught the attention of Mercy and Grace, "Such a large, majestic bird, yet so innocent a call..."

Silence always stayed close by Mercy and Grace, and never spoke, content to be who he or she was. Silence was silent.

They arrived at a fork in the path. One path ascended upwards to the right, and the other ascended upwards to the left. Enthusiasm called out to the others, "I would take both paths if I could."

This admission made the group laugh. "Why is that funny?"

Enthusiasm blushed.

Faith replied, "In life, when the road forks, we may only choose one path. We must choose wisely. One direction will lead us where we want to go, and the other will lead us where we do not want to go."

"How does one decide?" Peace seemed intrigued, "For this could be a valuable lesson for me to teach. This choice has always been my greatest challenge in life – the moment where a person can choose peace or conflict."

"Follow thy own heart," Love offered.

It was Faith's turn to speak once more. "Following thy heart is wise, provided the heart is guided correctly. We must look for signs and omens, and combine them with our interpretations and the vibration of the heart. With the right information, we can select the most fortuitous path."

They sat watching the rising sun and descending moon at the fork in the road. One path shot upwards to the right, and the other twisted upwards and to the left. Could they both be the correct path? They reflected on the journey, and searched for omens and blessings in their reflection.

"What path should we take?" Enthusiasm questioned, having the energy and desire to traverse both.

Mercy and Grace offered a recommendation. "We should follow the path of nature."

"That makes sense on many levels," Peace said, "seeing as all life emanates from the soul of the universe, which is directly linked to nature."

Faith looked up to the sky and noticed the eagle flying to the left. "I would have chosen right, but the eagle flies the left path. We all agreed to follow omens, to be guided by nature. Yes, the eagle flies left, so we shall go left. For the eagle is more that just an eagle, for he carries our spirits with him. If we align our spirits with nature, we can accomplish all of our goals and dreams."

"At the fork in the road, travelers and poets alike have written about the want to travel both paths," Love shared. "We cannot travel both paths and be one traveler, as Robert Frost said, so we must make choices. This is where our Guardian Angel comes in. They will give us a sign or omen. In this instance, the majestic eagle feels like that omen, for this bird does not inhabit these parts. We should therefore go forth expeditiously and soar with the eagle."

The eagle flew high, extending his wings to their full span of approximately nine feet. It kept ascending as if to leave, but would always descend back toward the Heart Sticks, circling the path leading left and guiding the travelers with its flight.

"Surely, the eagle guides us," Hope expressed.

The Heart Sticks traversed the left path. It curled around black granite, and jutted steeply upward. The trail was rugged and arduous. "In life, success often takes the longer path," Peace suggested.

They hiked in silence for the next few hours. The eagle accompanied them, flying up, then circling back again and again. This pattern held for the entire day, until dusk settled into night and they lost sight of the eagle. The entire group was worn down from the day's efforts, and they came to rest upon a flat rock. The plateau was exposed to the elements and not at all comfortable, but it was flat. Exhausted, sleep fell upon them quickly. The full moon illuminated the area like a night light.

Enthusiasm awoke first and looked around, viewing his sleeping mates. He walked left and right, unable to find a path. It was as if they had come to the end of the path and fallen asleep. He pondered waking the group, but thought better of it. "Let a sleeping stick sleep," he murmured, peering skyward in hopes of spying the eagle. He looked in all directions without luck.

One by one the other Heart Sticks slowly began to rise, as if called by the alarm clock of the sun's rays. By the time they were all up, the sun illuminated the entire sky.

They looked around, only to make the same discovery Enthusiasm had. They had gone to sleep on a flat rock and awoke unable to find a path forward. They looked to the sky in search of the eagle, without fortune or luck. "It seems, in our haste, that we made the wrong decision," Enthusiasm observed.

"When we get overly enthusiastic, we can often make the wrong decision. Yet how could we have ever known?" Hope asked.

"We should have went right," Enthusiasm grumbled.

A slight panic set in among a few members of the group. Faith spoke to them with authority in his voice, "We must believe in ourselves, and our choices. Let us search deeper for the meaning of our choice. Remember, we must keep faith."

The Heart Sticks searched frantically – left and right, up and down, north, south, east, and west – but were unable to find a way to proceed. With the wind picking up, the Heart Sticks discussed the possibility of heading back the way they came, but realized they could not locate the path from which they had arrived.

"How can this be?" Peace lamented, "We can neither find the way we came or the way we want to go."

"The eagle guided us. We trusted him and nature," Love said, "Such is my way. I always trust the unseen, for that is me – unseen and unheard, yet powerful nonetheless. It makes me smile when people think '*Where did Love come from?*'"

"We must read the mountain," Faith proclaimed, "and read the situation. We cannot find the path we have come from, and we know not our future path. The conclusion? We are now stuck here." Faith puzzled over their predicament. "What can we do from such a position?"

Mercy and Grace articulated, "How about we view the eagle as a spirit? Why would we allow nature to lead us? Why the eagle?"

Love replied, "We allow nature because it resonates with us in our souls. It is where we come from, and so it is our truest home. We ourselves are a part of nature from the moment we are born."

"Allowing the eagle to guide us made sense," Peace reasoned, "For we must have peace in our decisions and decision-making abilities."

"The eagle has many leadership qualities," Love interjected, "They possess powerful vision, and are fearless, tenacious high-fliers. For all their power, they remain gentle and nurture their young. That we followed the eagle may yet be a good omen."

Faith contemplated the others' words, "Yes, that is it, we must know our decision is correct. Once we do this, the universe will open up to us. Allow us to pray."

"Allow us," Faith began, "to trust our instincts and vision. We are one. We comprehend the concept of unity, where the ocean is one with the desert, and the sky is one with the land. We must be one with life. Now we call upon the eagle to provide us with divine passage from this isolated rock. Thank you mighty eagle! We give thanks in the hopes that you will answer our prayers. Amen."

Within moments, the eagle reappeared and circled above the Heart Sticks. The eagle briefly soared out of sight, but soon reemerged with seven friends. All eight eagles descended upon the rocky outcrop where the Heart Sticks prayed. Nature, prayer, Heart Sticks – all existed as one. They communicated by some unknown power. Having landed near the group, the eagles offered a ride to the

Heart Sticks.

Faith was quick to accept, yet Hope hesitated, "Is it safe?"

Faith, now hitched to the talons of the eagle, replied cryptically, "Is fear safe?"

Peace, looking into the eyes of the eagle who landed near him, spoke up. "I see peace in the heart of the eagle. The eagle sees peace in my heart. We must trust this omen is a good one."

Eight Heart Sticks hitched themselves to the talons of the eight eagles from the rock of isolation. How had the birds come upon the rock in the dark night? Their questions dissipated as they held fast to the eagles, who with every beat of their wings brought the group more in tune with the dual forces of nature and being.

The eagles soared higher and higher. Most of the Heart Sticks screamed in exhilaration, knowing they might never experience this sensation again. After all, flying through the air in the talons of an eagle was a rite typically reserved for the dead. The eagles flew up the side of Black Stone Mountain for what seemed like ages, and though in truth the group had only flown for the better part of an hour, such a journey still shortened their hike by many days.

The eagle transporting Faith landed first, and they conversed. The other eagles followed suit, landing one by one, dropping off Hope, Love, Peace, Enthusiasm, Mercy, Grace, and Silence, respectively. The Heart Sticks were on higher ground now, though still unsure of where exactly they were. They did know, however, that they were assuredly closer to the sealed stoned door.

They landed on a path that spiraled along the outer edge of the mountain. The path was worn, with light weeds filling the insides of the rocky crevices. That the path was worn meant it must have been traversed regularly once upon a time. On this day, however, the only travelers were the Heart Sticks.

Hope asked Faith, "What did the Eagle say to you?"

"It's funny… I never knew I could speak with an eagle until the opportunity arose. He thanked me, and all of us, for what we are doing," Faith told her, "He also said that he set us down on the backside of this mountain and gave us further directions: Circle the path, and we will come upon a perch overlooking the sealed stone door where the guard sits."

"Why could they not bring us closer?" Hope asked.

"They could have brought us as close as we wanted," Faith replied, "but this spot in particular was chosen for its safety – and to give us the best chance of success with our mission."

"The eagle mentioned something else," Faith continued, "He told me that he was created by the hand of God, and each of us are as well."

As the eight Heart Sticks adjusted to being on solid ground once more, the rising sun and the setting moon took each other's places. The moon retreated behind the mountain as the sun continued to ascend, lighting the way for the day's journey.

Their spirits buoyed by flight with the eagles, the Heart Sticks followed Faith as he strode forward onto the worn stone path. As they walked, chattering away to pass the time, a Heart Stick jumped out at them, causing a commotion.

"Who are you?" exclaimed Enthusiasm.

"Discipline," the brown Heart Stick stated his name loudly.

"Where did you come from?" Love asked.

"The same place as you," Discipline replied, "from the elements of the universe. You must be Love?"

"Yes, I am Love. How did you know this?" Love wondered aloud.

"You are one of my greatest confidants. For generations, the offspring of Discipline and Love have held a unique bond with one another," Discipline Stick explained.

Discipline was brownish in color, yet also seemed to blend into the pitch black stone. His body exhibited the properties of a chameleon, allowing him to blend in with the scenery around him. "Are you always able to be one with the scenery?" Mercy and Grace asked simultaneously.

Discipline laughed, "I am, yes! I am usually close by, often neglected, as few befriend me. When one gets to know me, we typically become loyal companions."

Before Discipline could finish his thoughts, a reddish, orange Heart Stick came running up to the group, smiling from ear to ear. Discipline greeted her, "Hi Joy!"

"You know each other?" Mercy asked.

Discipline replied, "Yes, we usually travel together, Joy and I. We are both considered elusive. We are always just around every corner, yet society often pushes me into a corner – except in places like the military, of course. But when that happens, Joy is not with me. We function best together, me and Joy, Joy and I."

Joy giggled, "Hi, everyone! Wow, there are so many of us! I shall enjoy the company." She injected a shot of energy into the scene with her presence, charisma, and smile. Her presence wordlessly gave exuberance and goodness to the group. Her vibrations exuded a rareified aura.

Love smiled at Joy, then spoke, "We are now ten strong, and close to the sealed stone door. We still need three more to unlock the door. So it is written, so it is said."

"They will be here soon," Discipline informed the group. "Allow us to keep going on our mission."

"Who will be here soon?" Love asked in reply.

Discipline responded, "The others; they will join us in short order. We must be who we are – nothing more, nothing less. Love, you must extol your virtue. The universe will take care of the rest."

"Where did you learn that?" Peace asked, but Discipline gave no reply.

Before them on the path sat a tree. That was odd, for no trees existed at this elevation. Upon the mountain's rocks no seeds could germinate, and no roots could grow. The group stopped before the tree. Enthusiasm whistled, "Now that is a sight!"

At Enthusiasm's words, the tree transformed into a Heart Stick and introduced himself, "I am Wisdom."

Joy howled with laughter. Discipline laughed loudly, "There you are my friend! Always shape shifting and transforming yourself so that the wise might see you, all while fools see only folly."

"What is happening?" Enthusiasm asked, now full of energy and frantically running back and forth.

"Once you all began to vibrate, you attracted me," Wisdom told them, "The wise know me, and Discipline and Joy are always close by."

It was with overwhelming excitement that the eleven Heart Sticks now walked the path to the sealed stone door. They were only two short of opening the door and freeing Legend Heart.

Wisdom began to guide the others in a ritual that would aid them, "Let us stand in a circle and hold hands."

From the moment he appeared, Wisdom had commanded the respect of the other Heart Sticks, and they obliged him now, forming a circle and holding hands. Eleven total now stood holding hands in a perfect circle. "Feel the power of one another," Wisdom instructed, "That is our greatest strength, our strongest power. Together, we need not force anything, for not even the smallest good will remain good with force. Using the power of Love, Hope, Peace, Faith, Mercy, Grace, Silence, Joy, Enthusiasm, Discipline, and Wisdom, we can unlock almost any door. Now, allow us to call for the final Heart Sticks to appear."

They stood in a circle of power, frozen in the moment, first waiting, then anticipating, and now fully expecting the final members of the group to join. As more members joined the group, Faith understood what he must do. He called out, "Let us go forth to the sealed stone door."

"It is known as the Door of Eternity." Wisdom said.

"Where did it get that name?" Hope asked.

"The where is not nearly as important as the how," Wisdom replied, "The name was given after Black Heart locked Legend Heart in. After he had done so, Black Heart cursed the door, saying *'For all eternity or until your brain is reprogrammed so your eternal heart becomes as black as mine'*. Black Heart then sealed the door, and ordered it guarded against any intruders."

"All the guards were given an assignment to defend the Door of Eternity, and word of Black Heart's deeds soon spread. For fools spread words like unabated fire on dry land in a hot summer without rain. Their words can burn and burn, scorching the earth forever – no matter what good deeds are done," Wisdom recalled, "It became an era where none knew the virtue of Silence. We are fortunate now, as Silent is with us today."

Silent Heart smiled, and cuddled next to Joy. Since Joy had joined the Heart Stick group, Silent had gravitated to her, and they had formed a fast friendship. Joy spoke for him, "The tongue can be the most dangerous organ."

Thanks to Wisdom, the truth of the stone sealed door became known to the Heart Sticks, who now referred to it by it's proper name. The group discussed the exciting events of the day so far. Faith beckoned them to resume their journey to the Door of Eternity, calmly offering his guidance and suggesting that "If we believe, the others will arrive."

At Faith's urging, the eleven Heart Sticks ventured the path to the Door of Eternity. Thanks to the gift of flight from the bald eagles, they anticipated that they would be nearing the Door of Eternity by nightfall. As they traversed the path, Hope asked, "How do we know we need two more Heart Sticks?"

With the arrival of Wisdom, the group at last had a master of knowledge. His gift for knowing what most did not know was one of his special qualities. Wisdom counted the group, counting himself last. "Eleven," he said, "We will need two more to unlock the Door of Eternity."

"How do you know that?" Peace asked. This was quickly becoming a pattern – first Hope would speak, then Peace would typically follow up with a question or response to Hope's inquiry.

Wisdom's reply was simple: "So it is written, so it is said."

There was silence among the Heart Sticks, as if they were digesting the totality of the great energy they had created and the special mission they were on. Love called out suddenly, "I feel the twelfth member is close by…" She gave a broad smile. "Yes, one of my best friends will be joining us."

Wisdom nodded in full appreciation of the moment.

Enthusiasm said, "Who do you mean? Will it be my twin Desire?"

Love did not answer. She simply smiled, knowing the answer – as Love does many times – before all parties are privy to such knowledge. She directed the group forward.

"Feel," Discipline said.

"Yes," Love replied, "we are each, in our truest essence, a vibration."

Wisdom smiled, adding "And it will be our collective vibration that unlocks the Door of Eternity."

As they were discussing essences and vibrations, what makes the core of a being, and who they themselves were in their deepest core, a voice spoke. A moment of silence passed – then it spoke again. "Did you hear that?" Enthusiasm asked the group.

"What did it sound like?" Mercy and Grace said at the same time.

Enthusiasm replied, "If I heard correctly, it sounded like the word Love."

The group looked for Love, who was away from the group. They found her eight feet above the stone path the rest of the group occupied below, peering around a malformed rock. It appeared that Love was speaking to someone. The other Heart Sticks stopped what they were doing and gazed up at Love. Grace quickly went to her aid, "What is it?"

Love finally replied, "Not what is it so much as *who* is it – our twelfth member!" Love waited a moment before calling out, "Forgiveness, Forgiveness...," It was as if she was calling into the day, into the rock, even into nothingness itself.

But Love was not calling into nothingness. Sheepishly, a large Heart Stick presented himself before Love and the group below.

Enthusiasm was awed, "That is the biggest Heart Stick I have ever seen."

"Forgiveness," Love called, and they embraced for a minute. It was clear that Forgiveness and Love had met one another before.

"How could it be?" Enthusiasm sheepishly murmured.

Love looked down the eight feet to the path below, announcing, "Heart Sticks, meet Forgiveness."

Forgiveness spoke, "Please, call me Forgive."

Love and Forgive made their way down from the rock overhang and joined the other Heart Sticks on the path. There, they began formal introductions.

"Forgive," Peace said, "How about we say who we are, where we came from, and one item about ourselves?"

"Yes, that is a brilliant idea!" Forgive replied before continuing, "My name is Forgiveness, and I was born in the town of Revenge. It was a town full of devastation. I was born an orphan, abandoned by all, yet with the Grace of God I defeated anger and resentment and became known as Forgiveness. My friends call me Forgive." With tears in his eyes he finished, "If I can make it out of the town of Revenge, anyone can."

"Wow, we can see that." Hope said. After a moment's hesitation, she continued. "My early days were rough as well, as I was born in the city of Despair. My parents were Sadness and Worry. I ran away at an early age. This is one of the first times I have felt family in my life – being with you all, that is, and falling in love with Peace."

Peace hugged Hope, comforting her, then said, "Well, I suppose I am next. My name is Peaceful, but please, call me Peace. I try not to think back to my childhood, and blocked out many of my memories. I grew up in the vicinity of Violence. At an early age, the sticks told me I was not like them, and left me to die on the side of the road. While there, an angel came to me and said '*Live, you are needed in this world. Go and be, spread thy true self.*'"

Hope was in awe of Peace's story. "Who was that angel?"

"I asked her," Peace replied, "and she said '*I am the Angel of Tranquility, and will be by your side every day of the journey.*' Then she reminded me once again to be true to thy self."

The introductions halted the hike as each Heart Stick spoke of who they were and where they were from. Each of their stories left the group rapt with attention, and hanging on every word.

Silence was moved, and spoke for the first time, "I am Silence – they call me Silent. I am from the city of Stillness, and my parents told me to go into the world and be the space between words, to be the constant of life. My life long dream was to meet Peace Heart," With that, Silence stopped speaking.

Peace, honored by Silence's words, went over and gave him a hug.

"Who is next?" Hope asked. The Heart Sticks appeared half-stunned. All this time they had thought Silence was a mute, but now learned he was raised in Stillness and merely chose to be Silent. Hope had to ask again, "Who is next?"

Love answered, "I can go next. Oh, but where do I begin? I was born in the Territory of Hate. It is one of the meanest places you will ever go. From an early age, I was bullied, for the sticks there knew I was different. From those shallow beginnings, I found deep self-worth, and decided to go into the world to find dark hearts and give them kindness, tenderness, warmth, and affection. Our mission is the crown jewel of my life work – to free Legend Heart, and make Black

Heart feel love."

The group remained quiet, waiting for Love to say another word, for each word she spoke was nectar to their soul, exuberance to their spirit. Enthusiasm eventually broke the silence, "My name is Enthusiasm. I am honored to be here. I grew up in the town of Boredom, where apathy, indifference, and laziness were everywhere. From a young age, my mother told me I was special and encouraged mc to go out into the world and be who I was, and that is what I do. I am thrilled to be on this journey and honored to be one of you all. Our travels fill me with exuberance, for this adventure is truly a highlight of my life!"

Grace and Mercy went next, and spoke separately while introducing themselves. "I am Grace." "I am Mercy," After giving their names, they spoke together, "We are twins, born to the parents of Disdain and Cruelty in the city of Neglect. At an early age, we realized we were born twins for a reason, and needed to stay together to draw upon each other's strength. Our first memory was of our parents beating us before the voice of God came to us and said '*Go into the world, and I will show you favor. For these transgressions against you will multiply in compassion, and allow you to meet*

78

Forgiveness.' On this day, we feel God's presence as we have met Forgive."

Forgive smiled broadly and went over to hug the twins, broad smiles upon all their faces. After they were done hugging, it was Forgive's turn to ask, "Who is next?"

Wisdom jumped upon a rock and said, "I will go. Where do I begin? My best friends as a child were the family of fools, and I was closest to Foolishness. We lived in the province of Madness, where they repeated the same follies every day. When I was a child, my mother guided me to read books. How I fell in love with those books… but they made me an outcast in the town of Madness, and at school I was bullied. Then I met Knowledge and my whole life changed. Knowledge taught me four-fifths were fools and told me that, for me to find my greatness, I would need to go far and wide accumulating insights, intelligence, and understanding. Over the next fifty years, I became Wisdom. I am self-made, born a friend of fools from a place of Madness."

"We love your company," Hope beamed, "Discipline, please go next."

"Yes," Discipline replied, "I grew up in Chaos. They were trying times, and I had a trying youth. I have a twin brother Order. I have been unable to locate Order, and have heard tell he is trapped in the Black Stone Mountain with Legend Heart. Those rumors are true. I watched with my own eyes as Black Heart's legion corral my brother and seize him. That is why I am here, to free him. This expedition is personal for me. It is said others have been captured as well...Happy Heart, Thankful Heart, and countless others. We are now hunted – each one of us – by Black Heart's army, so we must proceed cautiously. It is up to us to save the light of the world."

Discipline's words had a serious tone, and all the Heart Sticks stopped in their tracks, understanding the gravity of the situation. Wisdom finally spoke, "Yes, I heard Order is captured as well, and that is one reason I am here, but I also come because I seek truth and light."

A heavy cloud weighed on the Heart Sticks' souls until Joy volunteered her story to them, "It is urgent for us to free the other Heart Sticks, especially if Happy is in there. We grew up together in the city of Regret. All around us, sticks wallowed in sorrow, sadness, woe, and gloom. Our parents Bliss and Cheer told us we needed to go at an early age, and they sent us far away to school, never to return. They told us we could not fulfill our destiny if we remained in Regret. We really need to rescue Happy," Joy said, giving the group her best smile despite the worrisome conditions.

They had all introduced themselves except for Faith, and a pall of quietude fell over the group. They were about to prod Faith to speak when he began on his own, "It feels I am a long way from the City of Doubt where I grew up, and it has been many years. My parents were Denial and Reject, and it was from my choice to rebel against them that I became who I am."

"Yes," Faith said, "I am a dizygotic twin." The group murmured, and Faith continued, "Life is a journey of ups and downs, times to push forward, and times to rest. People often confuse me with God. They think you can only have Faith in God, but that is wrong. While that concept is important, what about faith in yourself? What about faith in this group?"

"I have faith in this group," Wisdom added.

"Yes, this is my zygotic twin, faith in self. So very important, faith in yourself, and faith in others, too, if you are grouped with others for a common objective," Faith said, "It will take all of us, all of our knowledge to liberate the light and free Legend Heart."

The introductions were complete, and the group walked along a rocky overhang where no vegetation grew, not even a weed in a crack. It was as if the shade prevented growth and seed germination; without light, the seeds died. They were close now, at the last bend before the entry plaza where the sentinel guarded the door. Wisdom called out, "We should regroup and make a final plan."

The twelve of them sat huddled, discussing their mission with renewed purpose, forging a strong feeling of togetherness now that they had formally introduced themselves. Unexpectedly, a voice called out, and a smiling purple Heart Stick appeared, saying, "Hi all! This is a magnificent day, and I am thankful to be here. My name is Gratitude Heart, but some call me Grateful – either is fine with me! Gratitude, or Grateful."

"The final key," Wisdom replied,"Yes, the final Heart Stick. We have everyone to unlock the door."

Faith rejoiced, "As it was written, it will take thirteen heart sticks to unlock the sealed door. The addition of Grateful makes us able to complete our mission."

The Heart Sticks were buoyed by their camaraderie, knowing that prophecy was on their side. They were confident as they sat quietly talking, when Love had a thought. "When will be the best time to carry our our mission?"

Wisdom replied immediately, "It shall be tomorrow night, when no moon exists."

"That sounds about right," Faith confirmed. "The scroll said to make the rescue when the night was darkest, and though I was unsure how to interpret what was written, I now see what was meant. Wisdom knows all."

Wisdom smiled, "One of the greats said, '*I am who I am for knowing I know nothing. Some think I know all, and some even think they know all, but such is the folly of fools.*'"

The day turned to night, leaving only a sliver of moon to provide a little light. The rock they were on was unprotected from the wind, and the lack of moonlight immobilized them. The Heart Sticks were exposed to the cold night air. Before long, they bundled together to create warmth. The group cuddled close together, feeling odd at first before realizing that they were one group, one mission, one being.

The wind kicked up with force, backing the group against a rock. Wisdom and Faith guided the group in finding refuge, and they positioned themselves against the rock, doing their best to shield themselves from the wind. Still the wind whipped at their small frames, chapping them. In the middle of the night, Love did the only thing Love knew to do. With all her strength of heart, she took the outer position. Suddenly, an amazing occurrence took place. Two bears came to Love – not hostile but friendly and gentle – and lay in front of her for the rest of the night. The two bears and Love weathered the wind until the morning sun began to rise and show its face. The male and female bears smiled at Love and ran off.

As the sun poked its crown above the horizon, the wind suddenly calmed down. Faith and Wisdom both thanked Love for her bravery, and asked if she was okay. Love responded, "When true, I am always good," She did not speak a word of the bears.

The temperature increased quickly with the rising sun. The Heart Sticks began to wake up one by one, and soon they were all awake. As if the plan had come in a dream, Wisdom asked all of the Heart Sticks to gather around. They huddled in a circle, discussing how they would outwit the guards defending the sealed stone door and free Legend Heart. A giddiness came upon the Heart Sticks as a plan materialized. The initial lack of a plan had created apprehension among some in the team, filling them with questions (how would they ever get past the evil guards?). Now however, with a plan in place, the Heart Sticks were energized and confident.

Discipline let his feelings be known. "My body is tired, but my heart is buoyant."

Concealing thirteen Heart Sticks became more of a challenge. They came around the last remaining barrier, Grateful noticed something peculiar. "Wow! That rock looks like a skull with crossbones." From then on, they referred to it as Skull Cross Rock.

"Below that rock lies the Door of Eternity," Wisdom informed the rest. "Once we turn around that corner, we will be upon a precipice above the guards."

"It is surprising they do not guard the high ground," Peace observed.

"Not many travelers can access the path from this position," Wisdom replied, "for we only did so with the aid of eagles. We are coming in through the back entry which gives us an advantage."

"Remember the plan?" Discipline asked.

"Yes, yes," Hope confirmed, "What will the magic word be?"

"We can use a magic word," Wisdom replied, "For this is a magical time."

"The time is now, it is always now. Take your positions and await nightfall." Faith instructed.

They all agreed, except for Grateful, and he remained. It seemed fitting. He had never formally introduced himself to the others. Grateful knew his role; he was the one Heart Stick who would remain in the present location.

"The magic word is this:" Wisdom whispered, "Harvest."

"Why harvest?" Hope questioned.

"Well," Wisdom reasoned, "it does not matter, but if you must know, we harvest the thoughts of our mind, so harvest it is. Harvest victory with victorious thoughts!"

The group dwelt upon the word. To get around Skull Cross Rock would take time. The trail summit consisted of thousands of massive stones, generational rocks that the universe had deposited millions of years before, in an era prior to Heart Sticks thinking complex thoughts and before members of civilization were able to properly utilize their minds. The Heart Sticks later became special for the ability to use their mind, to communicate and feel.

While waiting for the middle of the day, they discussed many topics. It was mentioned by Love, "It will be difficult to reduce my vibration to hate. Still, I will if it is deemed necessary to free Legend Heart, and the others who have since become trapped with him."

Wisdom whispered in the ear of Love, and what was spoken remained a mystery between them.

They waited until sunset before heading quickly to the top of Skull Cross Rock. Looking down from their perch, the view of the mountain seemed completely different. The sealed door from this view took the appearance of a frowning mouth.

As they peered below, they were taken aback at how many guards were on duty today. On the first visit a few weeks ago, there had been only one guard. Today that number had multiplied considerably. The Heart Sticks whispered to one another, and Wisdom made a final tally, "Seven," he whispered, "The time is now – harvest!"

Enthusiasm went first, running in full bore from the left; he was flanked by Peace and Hope. They climbed down rocks forming the left side of Skull Cross Rock and swung around the rock formation into the plaza. Peace screamed, with Enthusiasm joining in, "War! We declare war on light!"

The head guard was confused and said, "May I help you?"

Peace answered, "We were hiking when we decided that we want war on someone."

Enthusiasm chimed in, "Yes, we want some blood. How can we help you?"

The guard mentioned, "This is not the place, but we are with you. Do you want to help us guard the door while we capture more beings and vibrations of light?"

Hope looked serious, as if she were a different being entirely. "No, we can do it on our own. We will help guard the door if you allow us to torture the light travelers you find."

"In that case, I will take two of my guards with me and leave the other four with you, for this assignment is hard. We watch the door that never opens or shuts, except for the circle at the center – it turns black when we have a new vibration to capture."

"What color does it turn when one leaves?" Hope asked.

"We have never seen one leave. This is a one-way portal," the guard stated bluntly.

They heard something, and looked up to see a red Heart Stick jumping up and down, "I love you all!" the red Heart Stick shouted.

This sent all the guards into a frenzy as one of them called out, "It

88

is Love!"

The head guard called out, "Let us get her! This would be huge... if we captured Love, the world would become full of Hate. She is the most wanted Vibration in the Land of Sticks." Then he turned to the three Heart Sticks in disguise and said, "Three sticks of War, can you guard the door for us? We need all hands on deck to capture Love."

Enthusiasm was quick to speak, but Hope and Peace nudged him. Peace turned dark green, revealing a scar across his back. "Yes, we will watch the door," he affirmed, "as I want Love to be tortured as I was once tortured."

"Wow," the head guard exclaimed, impressed by Peace's bravado. "You really are one of us." He motioned to the other guards, "We have no time to lose. Go and get Love!" The four large guards and the head guard ran off toward Love.

One of them called out, "She is Black Heart's most wanted!" and they redoubled their efforts in pursuit of her.

Love took off like the wind, only slowing down occasionally so that the slow-moving guards would not lose sight of her. The game of cat and mouse was on.

The remaining Heart Sticks waited until the remaining two guards vacated their posts. A guard on the hunt called out, "She is fast! We need to trap her."

Love Heart circled around, disappearing for a moment, only to reappear moments later close to the guards. The head guard was lagging behind and breathing heavily. He called out to the two guards ahead and the two behind, "Let us trap her! You go left, you go right, and I will be in the middle."

Love displayed her astounding skills of agility and teleportation that allowed her to come and go all across the universe. She would be there one second, and the guard would say, "I have her boss!" Before he could grab her she would disappear, leaving the guard grasping at air.

"So close!" the head guard called out, "Continue pursuit," and the chase went on.

Love Heart seemed to enjoy the hunt. As she drew them further and further away from their lair, she called out, "You should know, never chase Love! One can pursue it, but it never works out." Her eyes formed hearts which smiled in delight.

By this time, the guards had been pulled far enough away from the Door of Eternity. Wisdom and Faith remained at the top of the skull, and Wisdom called out to the remaining Heart Sticks, "Our plan went better than anticipated. The time is now!"

The other Heart Sticks moved in unison, climbing down Skull Cross Rock to where the door was. There they joyously joined Peace, Hope, and Enthusiasm. Before Wisdom could instruct the Heart Sticks, however, Enthusiasm touched the black stone door. Immediately, a diagonal tan, orange color raced across the door.

Wisdom called out, "That is what we must do! Each of us need to touch the door. We all have a power to illuminate a section of it, and when we do it together, we shall unlock the door. It will take all of us."

Wisdom glanced up at Faith, and wordlessly, they acknowledged everything would be alright, though the plan's success still depended on Love and Faith Heart placing their hands upon the Door of Eternity.

Peace touched the door to the left, and a light green diagonal appeared.

Hope touched the door and a darker green diagonal appeared.

Grace touched the door, and a brown diagonal line appeared.

Mercy touched the door, and a violet diagonal line appeared.

Silent touched the door, and a white diagonal line appeared.

Joy touched the door, and a reddish, orange diagonal appeared.

Discipline touched the door, and a yellowish orange diagonal appeared.

Forgive touched the door, and an orange, reddish diagonal appeared.

Gratitude touched the door, and a purple diagonal appeared. He yelled out, "I am grateful to be a participant!"

Wisdom stepped up next. He glanced up toward Faith and nodded for him to come down. Then Wisdom touched the stone door, and an orange diagonal appeared.

The door was almost completely lit, needing only two more diagonals to open. Wisdom called out to Faith, "Have faith, for your time is now!"

Faith looked out over the rocky horizon, searching for Love Heart. Seeing nothing, he heeded the advice, and walked down to join the other Heart Sticks. Faith touched the door, and a light blue diagonal appeared.

The door was completely illuminated top to bottom, and was now only missing the middle diagonal. Anticipation and giddiness enveloped the Heart Sticks, for the mission was nearly complete. A sliver of apprehension began to swell, and Faith tried to dispel it, "Think of Love and, in this moment, send love to the enemy."

The Heart Sticks began to love those who hated and persecuted them, creating a strong vibration. As the vibration grew, they saw a vision of hearts falling from the sky like snow. For a moment, the Heart Sticks felt euphoria around them.

A shrill voice shattered the vibration. High above the door, on top of Skull Cross Rock, a shrill voice called out, "RED ALERT! RED ALERT! WE HAVE PERPETRATORS AT THE DOOR! RED ALERT!"

Faith called out, "Love your enemy!"

The shouting caused feelings of panic to arise as a rotund, rhinoceros-looking guard with a horn-like nose continued to shriek. Even as he yelled, the guard was walking down Skull Cross Rock to the door, ceaselessly calling "RED ALERT! RED ALERT! RED ALERT!" He only ever paused to catch his breath.

Wisdom encouraged the other Heart Sticks, "Remain strong in your purpose, and remember, *always* remember – you can never successfully chase love, only allow it to come to you or pass through you. Love is vulnerable, Love is free. Love is elusive and fleeting for those who know not how to Love."

Faith called out, "Love, Love, I am ready for you!"

The Dark Army began to appear suddenly from multiple directions, and the situation looked more and more dire by the minute. The Heart Sticks were *so* close to opening the Door of Eternity. They had all keys in the door to unlock it, needing only the vibration of Love.

As if out of nowhere, thirty-four guards appeared from all crevices of the mountain, under and around rocks near the stone door. "Where is Love?" Forgive mentioned, "Why have I always asked that question throughout my existence? Where is Love?"

The space between the group and the army grew smaller and smaller as the Dark Army Rhino unit – aptly named, for most of them looked like upright rhinoceros complete with horns for noses, slight eyes, and thick teeth – began to close in on the Heart Sticks. The Rhinos came closer and closer until the lead Rhino, who was still calling out, "RED ALERT!" was nearly upon them, within a few feet.

One of the Heart Sticks whispered, "This is the end of the line…" though who had said it remained a mystery in all the commotion.

Faith quelled the group, "Remain faithful! Love will show."

A sweet, melodic voice yelled suddenly, "I am here!", and all the Heart Sticks looked up. There was Love, upside down, dangling her feet from an eagle's talons. She looked down at the other Heart Sticks touching the Door of Eternity and the Dark Rhinos inching closer to thwart the attempt to free Legend Heart. Love did what she knew she must. She released her grip on the eagle and landed on the head of the Black Rhino closest to the door, bouncing off his shoulder to land within inches of her goal. She stumbled, but just managed to touch her hand to the door.

As Love touched the door, a red diagonal appeared across it. With all the diagonals full of color, the outer edge began to shine. The light on the edge was followed by a circle of light that appeared directly in the center of the door. The center circle turned yellow, causing light to emanate from the door and propel darkness away. Suddenly, the center circle's light exploded, knocking the Dark Rhino Army off their feet and away from the door.

From the center of the door, a majestic heart now escaped with all the stripes of the door and many other brilliant colors draped across it. The Heart floated freely. It had yellow ears and a yellow nose, and it was smiling benevolently. Wisdom called out, "Legend Heart!"

The floating Heart's smile became more grand by the minute, its eyes glistening with soulful light that immobilized the Dark Guards. One of the Dark Rhino yelled out, "I'm blinded! I'm blinded by the light!" Another Black Rhino concurred, "Me too! I cannot see anything!"

The smiling, floating heart without legs or arms began to speak, "Yes, I am Legend Heart. You have rescued me from the confines of eternal damnation. This is a glorious day! Allow the others to walk free."

Love, Faith, Wisdom, Silent, Mercy, Grace, Hope, Peace, Enthusiasm, Gratitude, Joy, Discipline, and Forgive stood away from the door. Legend Heart took one glance at the sealed stone door that had held him captive for so long. In a flash his smile eviscerated it, melting the Door of Eternity as if it were ice in the heat of summer.

With the door open, out walked Heart Sticks of all colors and vibrations. Happy Heart, Desire, Order, Resolution, Funny and Sunny, Romance, Cheerful, Fruitful… the list went on and on, as so much color and light that had been imprisoned was now free again to vibrate across the universe.

The Land of Sticks once again had balance. With the Heart Sticks freely roaming, light shined into every dark corner.

THE END

Made in the USA
Middletown, DE
21 August 2019